BY ALL MEANS

By All Means

Tim Love

ISBN: 978-0-9573847-0-5

Scan QR code for further title information

Copyright © Tim Love, 2012.

All rights reserved. No part of this work may be reproduced, stored or transmitted in any form or by any means, graphic, electronic, recorded or mechanical, without the prior written permission of the publisher.

Tim Love has asserted his right under Section 77 of the Copyright, Designs and Patents Act 1988 to be identified as the author of this work.

A Hotwire Short Story Collection
First published October 2012 by:

Nine Arches Press
Great Central Studios
92 Lower Hillmorton Road
Rugby, Warwickshire
CV21 3TF

www.ninearchespress.com

Printed in Britain on recycled paper by:

imprintdigital.net
Seychelles Farm,
Upton Pyne,
Exeter
EX5 5HY
www.imprintdigital.net

BY ALL MEANS

TIM LOVE

HOTWIRE

Tim Love lives in Cambridge, England, having lived in Portsmouth, Norwich, Bristol, Oxford, Nottingham and Liverpool. He works as a computer programmer and teacher, and is married with two bilingual (Italian) children. His prose has appeared in *Panurge, Dream Catcher, Journal of Microliterature*, etc., and has won prizes run by Short Fiction and Varsity. His poetry pamphlet, *Moving Parts*, was published by HappenStance in 2010. He blogs at litrefs.blogspot.com.

To all those who made these stories possible

Acknowledgements

'The Big Climb' appeared in *Staple*, 'Prague '86' appeared in *Transmission*, 'Method of Loci' appeared in *Horizon Review*, 'Definitions' appeared in *Under the Radar*.

Contents

Olga, December '76	11
The Big Climb	19
Late	31
Prague '86	41
Doors and Windows	51
Method of Loci	67
Dreams	77
Definitions	87
Fractals	95

Olga, December '76

Not so much as a postcard for three years, then she phoned me at eight one morning to say that they'd tied a pig to Battersea Power Station and would I like to come down. I asked what the fuck she's on about. "You'll see," she said. I had no essay deadlines so off I went. She was there at Euston, waving at me with both hands as I got off. "It's called Algie," she said, hooking her arm in mine, "you'll love him. Got your camera?" "Yes. How do we get there?" "District. We'll walk from Putney. Let's go!"

  We ran for the tube that was waiting at the platform. "It's like this for me all the time," she said, "you wouldn't believe how busy I am nowadays what with the City Farm and Mushroom bookshop. I did a frieze along the top of their window. Got there one morning and would you cop it—they'd whitewashed it over. They said they had to, they didn't have planning permission and it was distracting drivers. Serves'm right, they should be cycling. We could change here. No, Kensington's crap innit. Really crap. I get free eggs so I had them in me pockets once—Mike likes eggs you see—and the tube was packed, so you can guess what happened—knicker omlette. And hunt sabs. Got me picture in *The Times* on New Year's Day. But in summer I do the festivals. Manage to cadge lifts from one to the other, like stepping stones. Wibble wobble. I'm applying for Art Therapy jobs. Me dad gets me trips—he's a travel editor. I told you didn't I?—so I fly off to places, take pictures, make a few notes and he writes it up. Club 18-30 in Crete last time. Don't tell anyone. Saves him the hassle, and he pays me rent, the dearie. He's shacked up with the agony aunt—yeah really! Mum thinks it's a scream. She says she's sent some letters in about impotence but I bet she hasn't."

I'd always been the quiet one, and in the years since I'd left for University I'd learnt more words and had become even quieter, but I'm sure I must have said something in the train, probably about needing a degree to do therapy. She was as unselfconscious as ever, a whirlwind giving me no time to think. You can't be like that nowadays without being diagnosed as on some kind of spectrum even if you're an artist. I wondered how many people had taken advantage of her openness.

By then we were out of the station, heading west. "So what's it all about?" I asked. "Situationists I guess, but none of me mates told me nothing." When we got there, TV crews, Japanese tourists and chip vans were flocking, but Algie had gone. "It broke free," a guy told us, "it's heading for Heathrow." We hung around, joined in conversations. I found out that Algie was a pig-shaped balloon, a prop for Pink

Floyd's photoshoot for an album cover. Suddenly life made sense again.

"What now?" I said. She reeled off a list of exhibitions. I said okay. We saw Inuits at Battersea Arts Centre, took more tube trips, running up and down the stairs rather than taking escalators. On each journey she slipped leaflets beneath cushion seats: Vegetarianism, Battery Hens, a Performance Art festival—she had a canvas bagful.

"But why did they call it Algie?" I said in the ICA. "From *Rupert the Bear* I s'pose. Or was that Podgy? Anyroad, you know, the Pig. Capitalist power. Geddit? Lighter than air, tied to the means of production. Pigs might fly, but only if they're naked. Let's all go naked!" Outside the Serpentine gallery at closing time we shivered even fully-clothed, looking at the ducks sheltering against the cold. "Want to stay tonight?" she said. So we changed at Victoria for Vauxhall. In the High Street we bought some cider and a take-away, turned into a cul-de-sac of terraced houses. "We call it 'The Squat' but it's not really," she said as she undid a padlock, "Must have changed places twenty times this year. Broke into a few meself."

We ate in the kitchen at the back of the house, looking onto a few square yards of concrete. I'd expected herbs at least. We'd bought the *Evening Standard* and read that flights had been delayed, and that Algie had landed in a farmer's field. "They let it go on purpose, didn't they," I said, "A stunt." "Destiny more like," she shrugged, "Homesick. You know what? I'm whacked."

We went upstairs. "Mike's away for a few days," she said, opening the bedroom door. She switched on the TV, the only light in the room, the sound turned off. A mattress nearly filled the lino floor. I looked around for any sign of me—old tee-shirts, a photo—but the room didn't even look like hers. It was cold, colder than outside. She asked if I had matches, rummaged in a drawer for a box, lit the gas fire. It didn't warm the room. Close to, it burnt. Under the blankets I licked the salt of her neck, felt the excitement of discovery combined with familiarity, a sense of returning after a long journey. And then, when I thought we were just having a breather, she dropped off.

The fire was still a blue, muted roar. Maybe I extinguished it hoping the clicks as it cooled would wake her. Friends had never understood what kept us together. I think it was a simple matching of her excesses with my deficiencies and vice versa—the things I remembered, and what she forgot. She was as oblivious to consequences as she was of the past.

Three years before, we were welcomed a few days at a time at HQs and camps, ever the willing volunteers. I did press releases and pamphlets—"Intensity in Tent City" was my idea. She made rainbow Union Jacks and Union Jills. They were suspicious that I always kept a camera with me—they thought I'd been paid by the police to collect evidence—but even then I reckoned momentous events were taking place that were worth recording. All the same, I could never believe that there was any point in their protests. Our protests. If a new law was made, they'd break it, thinking they were being political, fighting for freedom. Personal hygiene as oppression. It seemed to me that the government had tricked the Brew Crew and Peace Convoy into isolating themselves in fields miles from anywhere, miles from the masses. Their rebellion served only to reinforce the status quo and amuse the tabloids. I grew cynical about Olga's heroes too—the Eco-warriors were first to volunteer to lie in front of bulldozers, but vanished when there was washing up to do. And it's strange how unisex fashions were always male ones, how the Ego-warriors bee-lined for the cute chicks. Even then I was using the past (usually American—they were years ahead of us) to interpret the present, and that made me regressive in their eyes. A Tory.

Well fuck that, I thought, and gave up fighting—fun for a summer but not a life.

Her arm was still round my neck. I lifted it by the wrist and elbow, placed it by her face. They'd teased her about her hair. She didn't spend long on it, it just looked that way. I took the weight of her knee and rolled from under it. On the TV, cowboys were riding together, shooting in the sky. I collected my clothes, dressed on the landing, and let myself out. The tube was still running so it couldn't have been that late. I took a photo as the train arrived. I still have it—no ads, no "Next train in 3 minutes" displays, no "Mind the Gap" announcements to joke about.

Looking back, it's easy to see Algie as a pretext, but even if she was going through a bad time, she was incapable of pre-meditated scheming. Something needed recording, that's all. My name must have popped into her head that morning and one thing led to another until she fell asleep.

If I'd have stayed the night we'd have been up

early next day to see them try again at Battersea. They patched up the pig. This time a marksman was ready in case it broke free. They got good pictures but the sky was boring blue, so for the album cover they combined the pig with the previous day's clouds. The pig, designed by Roger Waters, appeared at Pink Floyd's concerts. When he left in '85 he let them use the design only if they paid £500 per concert. The rest of the band added balls and a prick to it to get round the copyright.

But I didn't stay. I never stood in front of bulldozers like a toreador or did my shift in a tree-house to block the construction of a bypass. After completing my studies, I lectured at the same University on "Contemporary Sociology: Alternatives and Lifestyles". Later I built a tree-house in the garden for the kids, posted letters in their letterbox to make it real.

The Big Climb

In my early teens my imagination used to run wild wondering how dirty knickers ever ended up on pavements. Then at university I discovered launderettes and learnt how easy it was to drop the odd sock. Launderettes became part of my social life, only to fade away with marriage. Now it's time to introduce my son to them. He's excited by the whole experience—putting in the money, watching the flashing lights, leaning against the mustard-coloured MAYTAG machine as it vibrates.

    He's had a good holiday so far. The long train ride here was a treat in itself. I let him look after his ticket so he could give it to the man he called the ticket catcher. He had his own rucksack too, though all it contained was crisps, a Coke and a ball—mine had everything else. He seems happy but I don't know what will happen when my leave finishes and school starts again. The lights of our machine go off with a click.

"It's stopped Papa. Can we go home?"

He means the caravan. Though we've only been here four days, it already feels like home. It's my first time. I was surprised by the mod cons—we even have colour TV, though the reception's bad. Formica table tops, formica walls. No space wasted—hidden compartments everywhere. We could fit everything we've brought under the benches if we tried. I'd given him first choice of bed. He chose the top bunk-bed leaving me with the double bed in the next room. I'm looking forward to tucking myself in; it's been a long day.

"Yes, we won't bother with the driers. Come on, let's play cranes."

I lift him up and he empties the machine into our two rucksacks. We swing them onto our backs like real climbers and make our way up the paths—steep so that everyone has a view of the lake.

"Do you remember the number of our caravan?"

"One and eight."

Actually it's 180 but he's getting better. As we pass 179, Sid and Doris appear. It happens so often I think they must be on the look-out for us. We've come to know them—a kindly old couple who say they stay here each year.

"Hello Sam. Where have you been?" says Sid.

"Washing."

"All day?"

"No, not all day, silly. Papa and me went up hills."

"Show Sid and Doris your hill dance, Sam", I

say. He stands on one leg, arms akimbo and wobbles.

"It was a bit slippery up Priests Crag today."

"But I don't fall down at all", says Sam, "Papa bought me some climbing boots."

"You *are* a clever boy", said Doris. "We've been walking too. That's why we're hungry now. We're just going to get some chips. Do you want any?"

"We've eaten thanks", I say, before Sam answers. "See you tomorrow. Say bye, Sam." But Sam had seen something in the grass.

"Here you are", he says, giving the feather to Doris. "It's a present."

"Oh thank you, Sam."

"Come on", I say. He waves goodbye, turns, and we reach our caravan. While I fiddle with the lock he suddenly runs back down the path. "Sam, come here!", I shout but he's away chasing Sid and Doris. He stops, bends down, and continues running away. I rattle the lock one more time, then, still wearing my rucksack, chase him.

"Excuse me", he says when he reaches them, "you've dropped your present."

"Sorry Doris", I say.

"Oh it's alright love. There, Sam, I'll put it in my pocket. I won't lose it again."

"Now that's enough Sam, it's late! We've our big climb tomorrow so we need a good sleep."

"Up Ska Fell Pike?", says Sid. I nod. "Well good luck. It's a long climb but not a hard one. Keep to the paths and you'll be alright."

Back towards the caravan we go. I can hardly make it up this time. There's a knack to the lock that

I haven't yet learnt, so I keep turning the key and rattling the door. Finally inside, we close the thin curtains. Walking and swimming tires us, so his evening rituals are shorter here—pyjamas, hot milk, and a quick story. I lay his clothes on the bottom bed ready for the morning and say goodnight, wedging his door open with a shoe, keeping the kitchen light on. I lie on my bed and start a crossword. After a few minutes he starts to cry. It happens every night but I still go in.

"What's up?"

"Nothing. Goodnight Papa."

He'll settle down this time. Night falls quickly—a country darkness, intense but safe. Sam wanted to stay up when Sid and Doris told us that foxes roam here at night, but we're always too exhausted. I'm too tired even to read.

I wake early, put on the gas fire, make a coffee and sit on the corner couch of the lounge. Out of one window I can see the lake. Through the other, hills appear, first grey against the grey sky then I can make out walkers' paths, the odd sheep or two. Before long it's a bright morning. At this time of the year that can only mean frost. I watch birds swooping, collecting material for nests. Sometimes I hear them walk on the roof. Then a movement catches my eye. I see Doris topless, just out of the shower. She's bald. I guess we all have our private tragedies to bear. I can't help watching her prepare the breakfast. Then Sam screams out. I rush to him.

"What's wrong?"

"Papa, I can't see."

His eyes are all gunged up. Conjunctivitis I

suppose. He's frightened. "It's okay, don't worry, I'll just wash your eyes."

I go and wet two pieces of kitchen towel, one for each eye, and clean him off.

"Better now?"

"Yes."

"Perhaps you caught a germ in the swimming pool yesterday. But it's okay now. Come on, time to get down from your castle." He inches himself backwards down the shaky ladder. I leave him to sort himself out. He's settled into his new room and keeps it tidy. He has his colouring book, his cars and his Lego with him. I don't really know what he does when he's alone. It always seems a shame to interrupt him if he's happy.

I never used to look after Sam much—too busy at work. Perhaps that was part of the problem. Who knows? The social worker says that people sometimes want a break, that things get on top of them and they don't know what to do. So they go away without warning. The police had no news, they didn't seem interested. I phoned her boss at the library but they were as puzzled as I was. She had no close relatives—she's an only child, and her parents died before I met her. Perhaps that was the problem. She takes little bits of money out of the joint account. Not often; when she's desperate perhaps, just to let me know she's okay. But Sam never wants to talk about her and I don't want to push him. He'll talk about it when he's ready.

I look over at the next caravan again. Doris pulls off her beige showercap to release her bouncy perm. Sid comes into view, holds her from behind. They're too polite to ask Sam about his mother. In return I've never asked them if they have children.

Sam joins me in the kitchen, his shirt back to front. "What shall we do today, then?" I ask.

"Eat all our cornflakes up."

"Then what?"

"Climb and swim, like we always do. Then have chips."

"You can't swim today, Sam, not with those eyes". A shame, because the camp's pool is warm, open to the public. No splashing. No petting. I can watch the local girls, overhear their gossip. "Today, Sam, we're climbing Ska Fell Pike."

Breakfast doesn't take long. We leave the dishes in the sink. I do up his boots, then put on my gardening boots, still wet from yesterday. We pack two cans of Tango and some Mars bars into my bag and head up the path behind the camp site. One stile and we're into open country. We've developed a technique. He goes first so I can catch him if he falls, so no-one gets between him and the sky. He's got good balance for his age. Some five year olds I've seen can hardly even hop.

"See the sun?", I say, pointing back, "It's bright today and it's getting higher. Maybe it'll get to the top before us."

"I'm tired."

"We've only just started. Come on. Stay out of the shadows, they're slippery. We'll stop soon for a snack once we're up with the sheep. Why don't sheep slip Sam?"

"Because they haven't got any plasters."

"No. Because they've got special feet called hooves."

"And I've got special shoes called boots."

On the first flat section I carry him on my shoulders—we've a long way to go. We start singing nursery rhymes together—the Grand Old Duke of York, Jack and Jill, and then when we can't think of any more hill songs we start on Little Bo-Peep.

"See our tiny caravan?" I say.

"I can see *lots* of caravans."

"How many?"

"One and eight."

"More than that. Hundreds and hundreds. Ours is the one with the yellow roof, the one all the birds like walking on. Do you like this holiday?"

"Yes."

"We'll come here again when Mummy comes back."

"Yes. Look Papa, more sheep. They're running away. Where are we going?"

"Up. Up and up."

"I'm still tired. When are we going home to our real home, with Mummy?"

"Soon. Ouch". I slip over just when I didn't want to.

"Papa. You're covered in poo", said Sam, laughing so much that, despite his special shoes, he slips over too.

"That serves you right. You shouldn't laugh when people fall over. Mummy wouldn't."

He got up. "Well I'm not going to slip over

again." He starts jumping. "Papa?"

"Yes"

"It's all springy."

"That's the moss. Come on, help me up."

We continue on the trail. No-one's in sight. We start passing sheep, first in ones and twos baaing nervously, then little groups, the last of the frost in their shadows.

"Look Sam, lambs. They're having breakfast. What's a mummy sheep called?"

"I don't know."

"Ewe."

"Me?"

"No, another sort of 'you'."

"Where are the daddies?"

"In the pub."

"You're joking Papa. There aren't any pubs here."

"Yes there are. Just wait until we reach the top of the hill. Hurry up, I'm thirsty!"

"Is there a castle at the top too?"

"No. Nothing except grass and stones."

"And sheep poo."

"Yes, lots of sheep poo."

"Ewe poo."

He starts laughing again, a little too much.

"See behind that bump, Sam? There's a wall."

"Is it a castle? A broken castle?"

"No. It's a little place where the sheep can hide from the wind. It's called a pen. Sam, do you know what ewes write with?"

"No."

"Sheep pens."

"Why?"

"It's a joke. There are two kinds of pen you see."

"I've got lots of pens."

"Yes I know, but this is different. I've just thought of another joke. Why is Papa like the sky?"

"Because there are two kinds of sky?"

"No. Because they both have a son." He stares at me blankly. "Sam, I think we've walked far enough for the moment. Let's have our snack against the wall."

Looking up, I see that we haven't gone as far as I'd hoped. From now on the views would be boring: more of the same but smaller each time we look back. The lake is shining. Perhaps it will be a hot day after all. From now on endurance will be all that matters. But I have a feeling we won't make it to the top. Not this year. I take off my bag and we settle against the sheltered side of the pen and start eating.

"It hurts", says Sam, breaking the silence.

"What hurts?"

"This wall. It's itchy."

"It's a dry stone wall. It's got no mortar."

"What's mortar?"

"It's like glue."

"Has our house got mortar?"

"Yes. We'll have to go home soon you know Sam."

"Can we have chips with Sid and Doris?"

"No, I mean our real home. We'll go back on the train, and when we open our front door there'll be a pile of letters. One of them will be from Mummy saying she'll come back."

"How do you know?", Sam says.

"Because I know everything."

"Do you know where she is, Papa?"
"She's having a holiday."
"In a caravan like ours, with bunkbeds?"
"Yes, but with her clothes scattered all over the place."
"And cups of tea all over the place too?"
"Yes, and the shopping and washing not done."
"And the telly on all the time?", said Sam, "and her crying all the time?"
"Is that what she did, Sam?"
"Sometimes. And she forgot things. But I don't forget. I eat up all my food."
"What else did she say?
"Nothing."
"Did she ever say anything about me?"
"No. Can we look for her caravan now, Papa?"
"We'll try. What colour do you think her caravan is? What colour does she like?"
"Pink I think. Can we go there?"
"If you like."
"Where is it?"
"Well, first we have to go past the castle, then we'll have a pint of beer at the pub."
"Can I have Coca-cola?"
"Yes, and crisps if you want, and when we're at the top we'll look down at all the caravans. There can't be many pink ones."
"What number is it, Papa?"
"We'll just have to wait and see."
"Yes", he said, nodding slowly, "we'll just wait and see."

LATE

While I was warming up my take-away last Wednesday, the phone rang.

"Hi. It's Alan. Alan Parker."

"Oh hi", I said, giving myself time to work out who he was.

"Went to your parents' house. The people living there gave me your parents' number, and they gave me yours. Hope that's okay."

By then I'd remembered him. "Yeah sure. Long time no see. Must be ten years."

"How's it going?"

"Okay."

"Good. Thing is, well, Bill's dead."

"Bill? Bill Pearson? How?"

"Dunno. He'd been living in Scotland then got divorced. Met his dad in the street. Says he was buried with his mum in Milton cemetery last month."

Wondering what to say, I stirred the curry and took another sip of wine. We never were chatty, especially on the phone, though we were best friends once.

"Thought you'd better know", he said.

"We should visit, I suppose."

"His dad didn't say exactly where the grave was. It's a big place."

"Let's meet at 1pm on Saturday. It'll be like old times."

So here I am: Fratton Road on a drizzly winter's afternoon. The graveyard's not far away but I wanted to come here first. McIlroys department store used to be our Saturday treat. We'd chase around its three floors, have a laugh in the lingerie department, make the cosmetics girls giggle. Alan, Bill and I met here once a year after leaving school. We talked about the old days and took an annual photo at the photo-booth just inside the main entrance. It's all gone now—replaced by an office block.

Zigzagging down the side-streets, I see that the corner shops haven't changed though. I buy a bottle of cider, manage to smash it just outside the shop, go back and get another. Some streetlamps flick on; maybe it's later than I think. I keep going, taking gulps when no-one's looking.

The rain stops as I reach the cemetery. I phone Alan and go through the main gate. We used to sit drinking, passing round a bottle of Lucozade that we'd filled with cider. The big wire bins are crammed with flowers, the ones at the bottom rotting. Some things never change.

Still soggy, I sit down and pull out the wallet of

our photos. Sometimes we were solemn, our heads in a triangle, other times silly. It was my job to split the photos up, keeping the spare one for the archives. We were always together at school. When we streaked once they called us *The Three Bares*. Alan Parker and Bill Pearson were always together in the register and the playground, with me, the eternal hanger-on, smiling quietly in the background like Ringo Starr.

An old man and an even older woman pass, looking at every gravestone, ignoring me. I slip the photos back in my pocket, check my money and my watch.

Then Alan appears. I'm shocked that he's bald.

"Hi. You took your time", I say.

"Thought you'd be here hours ago. It's getting dark now. My kid's ill. I haven't got long."

"Sorry, the train was delayed. The grave shouldn't take long to find though. Let's start in the far corner—that's where the new ones used to be."

We walk past the old graves, looking left and right—urns, angels, but mostly tumbling headstones.

"So how did it happen?" I ask.

"Bill? I don't know. We haven't been in touch. You know how it is. Anyway, what have you been doing with yourself Colin? Sailed on Everest yet?"

"Why should I?" I reply obligingly.

"Because it's there!"

The old routine. In our first geography lesson Mrs Simms asked us what the biggest lake in the world was. Trying to impress her because she was so pretty, I'd stuck my hand up and said "Lake Everest". I've never lived it down.

"Actually", I say, "I tried Tobago last year. What about you?"

"CenterParcs."

"Never heard of it. And what happened to McIlroys?"

"Shut down years ago. Bad location. Suburbs. Not one thing or the other."

We carry on in silence for a while.

"These graves are in a state, Alan. Sad really."

"Someone died here last year."

"You don't say."

"Some kids were mucking about and a headstone crushed one of them. Serves 'em right. They have to put up danger signs now in case parents sue."

At the end of the main path the graves are more random, no paths to follow, so we wander. The fresh graves are scattered amongst the old ones. I have to concentrate.

"Colin, it's too dark", he shouts, "let's call it a day."

"It's okay, my camera's got a flash."

"We need floodlights, not a bloody camera."

"Shh. What's that?"

Chains rattle in the distance.

"They're locking up", he says, "let's get back to the gate, quick."

"We might as well finish the job now, Alan. We can slip through to the Seven Stars' garden."

He shrugs. We keep still and quiet for a while.

"I think they've gone now", I whisper, "Let's move. You go left."

"Hold on. Let's not separate."

"You're not scared are you?"

"No, but if we lose each other we're really in the shit. You can get done nowadays for being drunk in a cemetery."

"Relax Alan. In a few minutes we'll be sitting in the Seven Sisters over a pint. I've got the old photos."

"Like I said, the kid's ill. It's pointless looking any more, it's too dark. Some other time maybe."

"I just want a picture of his grave. We owe it to him, Alan, we're his mates."

"Well it's here somewhere. Why not take a picture of the whole place?"

I turn on my camera. The screen says 'change the batteries' then blacks out.

"Don't tell me—you've got no spares."

"I was going to get them on the way here."

"Let's just have that pint. This place is giving me the creeps. I think it's this way."

We dip under yew branches towards a row of houses, then follow the boundary wall. Where it used to be waist-high at the end of a beer garden there's now a fence topped by barbed wire.

"That's it. We're trapped", he says.

"I've got my mobile."

"So who are you going to phone? *Excuse me, is that the police? I'm trespassing. Can you help?* Look Colin, I've got a decent job. I don't want a criminal record. Got any kids yet?"

"No." And no partner, just a pokey flat, a job where I've been passed over twice for promotion, where my bosses are younger than me, where I can't leave because I depend on the company car, the company social club, and the subsidised groceries.

"Remember that camping holiday?" I say.

"Yeah."

I wait for him to finish his sentence. Instead he tramples down some nettles and continues walking.

"Bill woke up with a frog in his sleeping bag, and we had our first drink together—bottles of Watney's Pale Ale that Bill nicked from his dad's shed. We ate cornflakes like they were crisps."

"I'd forgotten about that", said Alan, "Poor old Bill."

"Yeah, poor Bill. End of an era. Hey, look."

Some wooden panelling had been kicked in. We squeeze through and find ourselves in an alley.

"Close thing Alan", I say, "thank god for vandals otherwise we'd have been in there all night."

"I'd better dash, Col, or I'm in trouble. The wife has a keep-fit class at seven. Look after yourself." He shakes my hand and turns away before I can reply.

I follow him for a couple of steps, look back at the hole in the fence, then stop. The trip had been a stupid idea. Alan and I never had much in common. I'd just been trying to do the decent thing, but who cares? Suddenly cold in my wet clothes I head towards the station, looking in the front windows of terraced houses. Families are preparing for meals. Across the road, two girls sit on a doorstep, smoking. They stop talking as I go by. The smell of fried food makes me hungry. I hurry on, hoping for a chip shop. A woman with a pushchair bashes into me. "Look where you're going", she says, "God, you're pissed. You should be ashamed of yourself". I jog away, rattling with change along Griffin Street past a patch of wasteland where I used to play. It's been turned into a park, the colours of the playground equipment glowing. Youths are sitting on the swings, laughing loudly. A few kids are playing football in the dark the way I used to. I start kicking along a carrier bag, dummying around lamp posts, then think I might as well do something useful, so I start filling it with rubbish—a Batman crisp bag, a pay-slip, a soggy scarf, a baby's bib, another bib, a seven of clubs, a squashed MacDonalds cup, a sticker of Alan Shearer. I drink the last of the cider and throw the bottle in too.

I pass the house where I grew up: 19 Anstey Gardens. It's the same as ever—even the bright yellow door hasn't been repainted. I don't bother asking if I can go in—I just want to get home. Alan and Bill lived in the next street, married in the same year, then both had their first child the year after. They talked about their kids a lot at our reunions. None of us were that brilliant at school, but I remember doing a lot of homework for them. They wanted fast cars. I wasn't interested in that. People think that unless you have a good job and kids, you're a failure. Marriage isn't all it's cracked up to be though. The sex is nothing special—it's like having lollies in the fridge. The married guys at work know more about satellite porn than I do. The parents moan about the school run, the endless lifts to sports lessons and birthday parties, the grind—never a moment's break. I've got my freedom. As long as I'm sober by nine on Monday morning, there are no questions asked.

The bag slows me down so I punch it into a hedge. When I'm drunk I feel I can run forever. I speed past the row of bus-stops, the queues mingling, and cut down side streets again, past launderettes I don't remember, their hot air billowing out as the doors open.

Reaching Marmion Road I stop, thinking I must have made a wrong turning. What's happened? Bombed in the war, it had been rebuilt too quickly, had become a slum and was flattened again — an unofficial car-park and dumping ground for mattresses. But now it's some kind of market closing down. I walk between stall-owners dismantling scaffolding that crashes down on either side of me. Amongst the bric-a-brac being packed away, one stall remains open, selling liquorice from around the world. When the terraced houses return, I carry on jogging. I'm nearly there.

The station's automatic doors open too slowly for me — I crash into them leaving a wet smear. My train's leaving in ten minutes. I suddenly regret throwing away the bag of rubbish; it would have been a souvenir, a bit of history. Then I catch sight of a photo-booth. I go in, draw the stupid little curtain, find some coins, get surprised by the flash. Then I wait for the photos to appear. They take ages. I'm dying for a slash and my train's about to arrive on platform 2. Finally they drop out, sticky from the machine. I'd forgotten to smile.

Prague '86

Jonas crossed in front of a tram with his customary sang-froid. By the time I'd crossed too, he'd already let himself into the block of flats and was furtively beckoning me inside. The smell of dust and mould stuck at the back of my throat as we climbed three unlit flights of stairs.

"We won't stay long", said Jonas, waiting for his aunt to open the door, "she's not very well."
I nodded. I'd become used to these unplanned detours, the mock secrecy. A bolt slid and a short, old lady appeared, wrapped in woollies.

"Ah, Jonas! Vchazet, vchazet."

"This is Mike, Aunt, my friend from England."

Without turning her neck she fixed her animated eyes on me. "Oh yes, yes, Jonas often speaks of you. You live in London, yes?"

"That's right. I met Jonas at Medical School. We played chess together."

"Chess, yes of course. Jonas plays a lot you

know. Well, come in. Please to make yourself at home. I am sorry for the room, I cannot clean it so often as I should." She held up her hands, gnarled with arthritis. Some teeth glowed silver as she smiled.

"We won't stay long, Aunt", said Jonas closing the door, "we are on our way to the Art Museum. I'll just retune your radios."

"Thank you Jonas. Mike, please sit down there by the window. It is only a little room so I move the furniture sometimes you know, if I feel sad. I have just had the kettle on. Would you like a drink? Tea?"

"Fine", I said and sank into the wheezing leather chair while she disappeared into the kitchen, walking stiff-kneed like a horse backing into a box. There must have been a dozen radios scattered about the room. Jonas began fiddling with a Bakelite set on the mantelpiece. "Why so many, Jonas?"

"The stations drift. She finds it difficult to retune them with her hands being so bad now. If she keeps them all on at once then at least one will be tuned right. That's what she says anyway. This one's a valve set that we found at a country market. She's always looking for more. By the way, you'd better call her Miss Kretchova — she's a bit funny that way."

He re-applied an ear to the set. I sat back again and looked around. There were high wooden dressers on every wall, crowded with trinkets, radios and family photographs. I recognised Jonas in a few; jaunty then later sombre, staring. Scanning the shelves my eyes caught on a bottle containing a dark-wood crucifix. I was about to get up and examine it when the kettle whistled, so I turned instead to the window. It was too small for the room and needed washing. Below, a web of tram wires jittered as a tram approached from the square at the end of the avenue.

Miss Kretchova returned, supporting with her forearms a tray which she slid onto the table, pushing aside the books and old newspapers.

"Let me pour, Aunt."

"Thank you Jonas. You know, Mike, when he was young we thought he would get us all into trouble. He would tell the teachers that what they were saying was wrong because it wasn't on the World Service. Remember, Jonas?"

"Yes, Aunt." She paused as a tram rattled past. "But he's a good boy to his Aunt Suska. Do you like Praha, Mike?"

"Yes, very much. I've been here almost a week now."

"So you've seen the Old Town and heard how we cruel Czechs pull the plug out on the Christmas carps?"

"Yep. Jonas has told me all about that." As he gave me my cup he threw me a cautionary glance then retreated to a radio with fretwork of a palm-treed desert island over the speaker. He turned it down low then rushed on to another. The room was filling with soft music and mutterings. "I was looking out of your window while you were in the kitchen Miss Kretchova. The square down the road seems busy."

"October Square, yes, I often watch the people there, around the... oh Jonas, socha? ...my English you know, it is not so good." She lowered herself painfully into a chair by the table. I saw how thin her white hair was.

"Statue", said Jonas distractedly.

"Ah yes, yes, around the Lenin statue. It is very sad, you know. I knew the artist who made it; Vladimir Stropoff." She reached for a photo beside her. "I'm sorry", she said, her voice trembling, "you must think me a silly old woman, but they were good times for me. It was in '68. You know what happened in '68 Mike? So often the foreigners they forget."

"The Prague Spring."

"Dubcek was a Slovak, we knew nothing about him. We didn't know what to do so we just went on like usual. I was a journalist then and suddenly they said there'd be no censorship. Of course we thought it was a trick at first, but yes, it was true because they told us all about the show trials. I remember how all the foreign journalists came to visit and I showed them around the Bierkellers of Old Praha." She smiled at me. "Well, we knew it couldn't last. We filled our larders, we knew what would come. But I mustn't go on, must I?"

I lowered my cup. "Oh please do, I'm fascinated."

"Well, they came and they censored the word 'invasion' and many hundred more, and Dubcek reappeared in Moskva to sign the new protocols." She raised her voice above the sudden static. Her accent strengthened. "They asked poor Vlado to make a statue of the Lenin. I was living in Mala Srava then and he used to come around with a jug of beer. He couldn't decide what to do. He thought of showing Lenin with a hand in his trouser pocket, playing with himself, but he knew he wouldn't get away with it. If only the statue wasn't so big, poor man. Many workers, they had the day off when the statue was...", her head dipped a moment, "oh, when they had a ceremony and there were Russian soldiers everywhere. Koblakin, the Russian foreign minister even shook Vlado's hand. Two days later they found Vlado dead. It was the shame you see, Mike. His own people walking past it every day. Is the tea alright? You must have some beer. Jonas, take out a jug and get some beer from Schlossel's."

"No Aunt, we've got to go. If we don't go soon the museum will be closed."

"You have seen the Jewish Quarter? The clock which goes backwards?"

"Yes, we went yesterday", I said.

"Then you must go to Terezin. It is not far away, not nowadays. See how the Germans treated us. They lit a fire in the yard of the camp in winter. Some of the young Jews, they ignored our warnings and slept out in the yard. Each night they made the fire bigger then suddenly poof! there was no fire at all. Hundreds died that night you know." She began blinking rapidly then turned towards the window. "Unveiled! That's what you say, the statue was unveiled and there were Russian soldiers everywhere. Koblakin—"

Jonas cut her short by blaring a radio. "We have to go now, Aunt."

"No, wait! You will think we hate everybody. It is just not true you know, whatever they say. Yes, we hate the Russians. We hate the Poles because we have to send them our meat, and everybody hates the Germans. But wait and I will tell you a happy story." She bent double to push herself from her chair, scuttling into the kitchen to get a jug which she pushed into Jonas' arms. "Now take this, Jonas. Go down and get a litre of beer."

Jonas snapped a short Czech sentence. Her face turned from joy to sadness like a mask, leaving the burning eyes intact. She stood there, head down, jug hanging from an elbow while Jonas turned the radios off then took my cup from me. "We're going now, Mike."

I said goodbye to Miss Kretchova but she didn't reply. Led by Jonas I skeltered down the stairs into the street. I couldn't make out which window he waved at, let alone see her face. We continued our walk towards the square. The city was grey, left out in the rain too long. Schoolchildren were weeding the flowerbeds around the statue as we crossed into Ulfm Street. Jonas darted off the pavement to avoid some scaffolding. "This has been here a year now. It was put up soon after I returned. They have done nothing. Nothing!" He thumped it, leaving a rusty stain on his hand. "Soon they will take it down and move it somewhere else. In America they would call it modern art." He hopped back onto the pavement and waited for me to catch up. "I'm sorry about my aunt. I should have told you."

"It's okay, my gran had arthritis too, it doesn't worry me. In fact I wouldn't have minded staying longer. She's a colourful character. It's a tragedy her lover died that way."

"Lover! You mean Stropoff? No! She was twenty

years older than he was. She interviewed him once, that's all. It was her last assignment before the purge. Stropoff came round a few days after, begging her to withdraw her article, but it was too late. No one employed her after that; she'd taken too much advantage of the freedom. She's never got over it. And in case you're wondering, she's not a Jew either. We have Jewish friends, we all have. She picked up a story here, a story there."

"Her English was good."

"Yes, word-perfect. I had to bring an Austrian friend here a few weeks ago and she forgot the word 'statue' in German too." He stopped for a moment to pull out a handkerchief and wipe his hand. "I shouldn't be so angry with her, I know she can't help it. It's only that if the wrong people hear her, they might believe it all. Today was the first time she mentioned Koblakin. I will have to ask mother about that, look it up. I check everything she says. And then we will have a game of chess. It's been a long time."

We passed through Old Prague, its cobbles worn smooth as crocodile skin. The streets were nearly empty. Looking down an alley I saw a grey-coated soldier in a silent-movie clinch with a blonde. Away from the trams and crowds, the pulse of the city had dissipated into the crooked alleyways, replaced by the constant presence of the castle which I had come to use as a landmark. I instinctively looked out for it between the rooftops while Jonas, head down, hurried on ahead.

Doors and Windows

Carl calls me to the hall as I'm clearing the kitchen table after lunch. "I have to go, Mark", he says, picking up his prepared rucksack and walking out. He doesn't wait for a reply. He doesn't even shut the door. I do that, then return to the kitchen, finish loading the dishwasher, flick a switch ('half load'? Yes) and sit at the table, aimlessly shifting the transparent salt and pepper mills around. It's not pride that stops me chasing him, but lack of surprise.

I'd tried so hard this time, taking the initiative rather than drifting. I think my holiday suggestions were what scared him away; an unforgettable summer cruise down the Nile was too much of a commitment. Of course I should rush down the street, beg him to stay—*please Carl, just a week, I'll change, I really will, Carl*—but he's too far away now, so I slump as if in an induced coma.

Summers seemed so much longer when I was small. Each August we'd set out on a sweaty three hour drive to Wales. When mother accelerated up the short cul-de-sac, the sky with its huge clouds enveloped the rented cottage. She would turn our trusty Morris Oxford into the pebbled drive and brake hard, spraying stones onto the lawn. Father, worried that they'd damage the lawn mower blades and we'd lose our deposit, would get out and lob the pebbles back, levering out the embedded ones with his pen-knife. Their holiday arguments concluded in various ways but always shared the same beginning. If they forgot to unlock the front door I'd wander down the road.

Two other houses were nearby: a thatched cottage, and on the other side a smaller, older house that seemed to have been lifted from a terrace and dumped on wasteland. The cottage was painted white with red shutters, and little flowers climbed around the front door. Rosemary's family was usually there. They were posh, from Manchester. My mother wanted me to play with Rosemary, I being a shy boy and she an only child too. I saw little of her parents when I was in their house. Her mother would leave snacks in the kitchen then disappear upstairs. Rosemary had a wigwam; red canvas with clear plastic at the top. We spread the canvas on the grass, fed six bamboo poles into loops and set up camp in her back garden, which seemed pointless to me because we had no bows and arrows. She offered me corned beef sandwiches, which I'd never tried before but I thought I'd better eat them. Then she wanted to play doctors and nurses with her new doctor's kit. Feeling her stomach, I was shocked how different her belly-button was to mine.

"Now it's your turn," she said, "My mother's a doctor. She earns more than daddy does. What does your mum do?"

"Oh, lots of things."

I lay on my back looking up towards the light at the top of the wigwam, my sandaled feet sticking out cool in the breeze. I felt her fingers on me and started to feel sick.

"I'd better go," I said, sitting up suddenly.

"Did I hurt you?" she asked.

"No I've just remembered I have to go home. See you tomorrow."

I dashed down the road to my front door, not knowing how much longer I'd last. A flush of sweat came over me that turned cold and clammy. I was about to knock when I heard my mother inside, crying. I ran to a bush, pulled it apart, dipped my head and spewed purple and red vomit. I'd seen a dog sick like that once. I took some deep breaths. My legs felt weak as I walked round the side. The outhouse was padlocked. I rested my brow against its cool window and looked in, hoping to see mice scurrying between the sacks and garden tools.

"So you're back Mike," shouted my dad from the back garden. I wondered if he'd heard me being sick. I looked at my feet in case the sick had splashed there. I'd got away with it. "Your mother doesn't feel very well. Shall we go for a walk down to the stream?" I didn't want to disturb my mother, so I said yes. After five minutes, I collapsed and he had to carry me back. Mother was still crying, so I waited outside, offering to help dad search the lawn for stones.

Usually though, the walks to the stream were the best part of the holidays. We'd carry picnic hampers across the rolling countryside, sheep parting for us. My father always took his Brownie camera in case we found an interesting rock formation or a gnarled tree. Mother and I would have to pose, trying to appear oblivious to the main subject. He had a book about orchids. Sometimes we'd head for boggy land, sometimes bare slate outcrops, depending on which orchid he'd decided to ruthlessly hunt down. The photos of those were always blurred, the camera too close, and of course he daren't let himself pick one. We crossed streams wherever trees had fallen across. One intact tree was so big that its branch reached all the way over, too high for me to be allowed to walk along it. I hung beneath, my feet barely above the water. My arms were aching before I was half way across.

"I'm going to fall!" I shouted.

"Just sway," my father said, "forwards and backwards, then when you're going fast enough, let go. You'll reach the bank". I tried, but splashed in. Mother was furious.

Our parents calibrate our gauges of normality. I thought all fathers wore bright Trinidad shirts on holiday, or plus fours, and that they did the cooking. He loved taking over the kitchen, producing foreign dishes that mother and I had to battle through. I thought all mothers cried. The strange people were Rosemary's mother, who went to work, and George who shouted poetry. He lived in the other house. He'd sometimes say Hello as we passed. My parents replied but rarely stopped. His curtains were always drawn and I wasn't supposed to go inside. One day I was sent to buy some milk. He was on his doorstep, glass in hand, smiling at the sky.

"D'you like chemistry, my boy?" he asked. I looked like that sort of kid—short-sighted, glasses. As I approached I could smell his drink. He led me to his front room. My eyes had trouble adapting to the dark. There was a thick atmosphere, syrupy like his breath. The walls were covered with bookcases, books thrown haphazardly on them. Blip-blip sounds were all around. I saw glinting glass containers on some shelves; tubes and bubbles.

"Dullun my boy," he said, picking up a book and holding it open at arm's length, "Dullun Thomas, he's the master. Met him once you know". I nodded. He replaced the book. "So, here we are then," he said, spilling some of his drink as he gestured, "Satan's cave of shadows. Lived here all my life. If you've got a good brain you don't need no universities. Remember that, my boy". I was getting hot. My glasses were slipping down my nose. My parents would be wondering where I was. He tapped a demi-john. "Elderberry, from my own trees out the back. My father planted them. Go on lad, try some. It'll make a man of you."

"I'd better not."

"Don't take any notice of that father of yours," he said, and set off across the room, bouncing up and down, loose-wristed, nose in the air, chanting "The mower will break! The mower will break!" Then he laughed. "Never seen such a stuck-up old fanny.

Look, seeing as it's your first time I'll get you a proper wine-glass like mine". I followed him out to the hall. As he swayed towards the kitchen I made for the front door and ran home.

"They've run out of milk," I told my mother, breathlessly, "they said to come back later."

I was ten the last time we went. Rosemary's cottage was empty and George was more reclusive than ever. I spent many hours alone by the stream. I wasn't always a solitary child. I grew to be one through habit. Once alone, I began to notice things I hadn't seen before, and became attached to those pleasures, sitting so still that the wildlife came to trust me. I saw my first kingfisher and caught sight of my only otter, scampering behind the bared roots of a willow. After the storms that winter, there were more fallen trees than ever. I could peel off their thick bark in sheets revealing a mass of wood-lice; some grey, some brown, the biggest ones silvery.

After that year my mother couldn't afford the rent so instead I spent a week each summer with my father. He'd moved down to London. If we hadn't met for a while we'd start by flipping through the photo-albums, which didn't take long because of his one-film-per-holiday limit. He never talked about why he'd gone away, he said he'd tell me when I was old enough to understand. He seemed happier there, with his new set of friends. He died before he thought I was old enough, but my mother had dropped enough hints by then about how you can never really know a person until you start living with them. And even then, she said, you can never be sure. She's as happy now as I've ever seen her, back in her home town working in an old people's home though she's older than many of the residents. When I visit she shows me off—"He works with David Attenborough, you know." Then all the old ladies say what a nice man he is, and ask if I'll be bringing my family next time.

People say you only become a man when your father dies. Others say you first need to become a father yourself. I had the first glimpses of my future on those holidays. I used my freedom to choose solitude, needing others only briefly, when I was lost. The older I become, the more my life seems to have budded from those holidays rather than from home. Each August we continued from where we left off as if the rest of the year didn't exist. My memories of Rosemary are usually eclipsed by memories of university where I retreated from women into alcohol. But now, with the dishwasher swishing into its next phase, I can reach back further, understand more. My father's spirited hikes became my obsessive stake-outs, an apprenticeship of sleeping bags, thermos flasks and note-writing with frozen fingers. Working freelance on nature documentaries gave me a new source of friendships, though they never lasted long. I had to learn from those around me, but my colleagues were inexperienced in love, my kind of love. I let myself be guided by cultural conventions, finding it useful to swot up on the arts and subscribe to mailing lists—that two men should go to the opera together or visit a gallery is nothing strange, I belatedly realised. Alas, I've never had much of a liking for the Arts.

Professionally I progressed from badgers to the Serengeti. I moved to London, meeting Attenborough in editing rooms sometimes. If asked about me, no doubt he'd say he admired my work, though I suspect he couldn't put a face to the name. I found out more about him from his autobiography than from canteen chit-chat. When you see him on TV in the tropical canopy you don't see my hours of patient preparation, you don't see how he's helicoptered in, does his bit then is whisked off back to his air-conditioned hotel. Continuity's a myth created in editing rooms, but it has to be meticulously planned.

There are places famous for change. People go to Montmartre, Berlin and New Orleans hoping to feed off the vibes. I feed off more private sources. If I could have a wish, I'd like to ask Rosemary and George what they thought of me then, before nurture had covered nature's tracks. Perhaps Rosemary is famous now. Most likely she doesn't remember me. And yet there have been those who cared — older men mostly. They seem to sense something about me. Perhaps George sensed it. Certainly Bill Thompson did. Strange, I haven't thought about Bill for months. He'd introduced me to the gay scene, stopped me making a fool of myself. In return I'd sometimes spent the night with him. I knew he had others, but in those days we all had. The last time we talked we were having breakfast at his place. We both had terrible hangovers, but only I had a job. We'd argued about who'd have the remaining coffee until I filled a cup and stormed out with it.

I've lost his cup, and his address. All I remember now is that I used to get off at Aldgate to see him, so off I go, just like that, even before the dishwasher's stopped. I'm shocked by my impulsiveness. I'm the type that prepares aphorisms and lovingly polishes memories. Carl hated that.

On the tube, I wonder what I hope to achieve, whether Carl will change his mind, what I should say if he phones. I'm good at starting things, bad at judging the pace of relationships. I'm a quick learner, though I'm just as good at forgetting. In truth, I've many weaknesses. If they ever ganged up, I'd be beyond hope.

Out on the High Street I'm still lost. I take a left turn and let my feet lead me. Along Whitechapel Road I go, then left again, through the market. Between the stalls I see a glove shop, a cheese shop whose window display has teddybears in national costume, a delicatessen where a solitary worker wipes a marble board round and round. Between the shops, open doorways leading to stairs, pinned up notices in the passages. My spirits rise when I see the Lavender Arms on the corner. We'd often had a quiet drink there. The hanging baskets, recently watered, are dripping noisily. I feel carefree, younger then I've felt for years. I avoid the puddles, pass the posh houses, and his tower block comes into view. Rain has darkened the concrete on one side, as if a dog's pissed down it.

The place has been modernised—it now has a

security door. I can't see Bill's name on the panel of buttons outside. I wait for someone to leave, slipping in before the door swings shut. A notice on the wall reads *Be a Good Neighbour. No Parties*. Someone with a marker pen has changed *Parties* to *Panties*. Details begin to return: that he was on 13th floor (how could I have forgotten?) and that he lived next to the lift. Up I go. I remember my first time here, a door into a new world of seductive, working-class squalour combined with displays of artistic sensibility. I remember the smell of leather. I knock. I remember the excitement of not knowing what would happen next. A boy answers. Clean-cut — could have been me years ago.

"Is Bill in?" I ask, "Bill Thompson. He used to live here". The boy stares at me for a few seconds. Long eyelashes.

"I'll see if I've still got his address."

He goes into the bedroom. From the doorway I look around. For a moment I'm amazed — there's a new window with birds flying across. Then I realise it's a big flatscreen TV. The room's tidy. Tasteful. A roll-down blind depicting Chinese erotica. A Marlon Brando poster, cap at a jaunty angle. A photo of some black footballer. A CD cover open on an expensively small hi-fi. I belong to the last generation that had to waste their formative years learning how to become inhibited. The world changed around me while I was stuck in adolescence. I need to go back, pick things up from where I left off, otherwise I'll just keep repeating myself, sitting in kitchens. Perhaps Bill's already dead. The boy's so young though—maybe my journey here isn't wasted after all.

David Attenborough appears on-screen. No sound. I don't recognise the clip. I study his mannerisms, his intensity. It's true that you can't take your eyes off him.

"Sorry," the boy says, returning with a towel to dry his hair—I hadn't realised it was wet, "I must have junked it. Was it about something important?"

"Well yes, rather."

"Could I help maybe?"

"Perhaps. Might I come in?"

I enter before he has a chance to reply. He closes the door. Round it are hung several paintings.

"Like them?" he says, "Great aren't they? Like sunflowers done by Pollock. You know, really spacey."

"You're having me on," I say, "That sixties jargon. You weren't even born then."

"I got them from the street market. I'm into retro at the moment."

"Ah, I'm a bit behind on that."

Is he flirting or making fun of me? And why am I playing along? I walk to the window. The nearby flat roofs have railings and potted greenery now, sometimes even sunbeds. The window box is in flower, a garden gnome smiling back at me. Poking out of his trousers is a huge erection.

"Was Bill a friend?" the boy asks.

"You might say that." I turn towards him, taking in the room. "Have you been living here long?"

"A few months. My mother said she'd pay the

rent until I got myself established. She's travel editor on the *Standard*. I'm a painter. I rent one of the studios under the railway arches."

"What do you like?" I ask.

"Late 20th Century American. I guess you'd call it modern art."

"Is that a Rauschenberg?" I say pointing to the largest painting.

"No. My father's. He died 3 years ago. AIDS."

"Oh I'm sorry."

"It's okay. It's amazing he lasted so long. He got it when it was GRID."

"A father's a son's window. A son's a father's door."

In the resulting silence I look to the screen. Attenborough's in an old library, flicking through a book of watercolours protected by tracing paper—Dodos, Great Auks. He's wearing surgical gloves. I glance at the boy. He's watching too. I'm beginning to think that those eyelashes aren't real. Would he be impressed if I mentioned in passing that I'd lunched with the great man himself?

"There's an exhibition of early Rivers at the Whitechapel," I say, "His drawings. I'm told they're interesting. Want to see them tomorrow? It's open on Sundays."

"Okay then. But not the evening; I work at a restaurant."

"See you there at noon?" I turn away to hide my blushes. It was too easy, always has been—relatives often said I had my father's looks. If only I'd realised earlier.

"Okay then. I'll bring Bill's address if I find it".

I open the door, glance back and say "Thanks" before leaving. The lift's still there. I get in and press the button. Nothing happens. I realise I don't know the boy's name. I press again. The door closes and the lift moves, smooth and fast. For a moment I feel weightless. Tomorrow morning I'll catch the first train to Wales.

Method of Loci

On the train yesterday I had such a good idea that I thought I'd never forget it. By the time I'd found a backstreet hotel it had gone. Today I'm on the return trip, hoping that the idea will come back to me. It just has, in the same place as before. I start writing.

It's not the species with the richest range of noises which developed language, but those which used gesture. In our brain the areas controlling gesture and speech are still close. So it's no surprise that Greek orators remembered speeches by associating each part to a room of their house, imagining they were walking around it. And actors recall best the speeches made when they're moving and gesturing. Language began with a spatial component — more dance than song. If we purify language, we restore gesture and arrive at poetry with its ritual and rhythmic repetition — something that points rather than arrives, capable of referring to things beyond reach, making transcendence possible.

Forgive me. I've forgotten to say where I am. I'm actually in a train leaving Rabat, the air conditioning breezing into my face. I enjoy travel. I use cities rather than rooms. The content of my life long forgotten, historians will read it as a hollow quest. The woman opposite me is about 30. We introduced ourselves while the train was in the station. When the station-master, proud in his buttoned uniform, unfurled his flag and blew his whistle like a star-struck referee, straining steel gathered to a single tone, and the train choochooed like a child, throwing out balls of cotton wool that stuck to the pure blue sky. We shared for a silent moment the romance of steam, then carried on chatting about property prices in London. Now we've agreed on another silence. She has very mobile eyebrows. That's what leads you to look at her eyes—currently closed—which are blue/grey, strange in a brunette. She has the complexion of a blonde too—blondes get stared at here, so maybe she's dyed her hair. She's modestly dressed, though if you know where to look you'd know what she's trying to show off. She said she worked in the embassy. I said I'm trying to establish a logistics network for hi-tech importers. I also said, to make things easier, that I was unmarried. "Me too" she replied, as if this Dickensian coincidence bound our fates together.

Beyond the points and crossings of suburbia the rhythm settles. The train gains pace past the shanty towns that cling to the tracks. Every so often we pass someone standing by the line like a sentry, their blank face inches from our window. Sometimes there are stations, but we don't stop. No houses near them, not even a path leading away—just a platform and a sign in stylised Arabic. I can recognise a few words now; *sidi*, meaning water-hole, appears on many platforms. In Rabat I bought a few things in the market without sounding too much like a tourist. Visits to Waitrose had prepared me for the range of fruits but not their size. I didn't need to point, I already knew some names. In the ninth century Arabs brought the first oranges from South-east Asia to Europe, naming them after the colour of these desert sands — Naranj.

"I must have dropped off", she says.

On the journey from the window to her face my eyes flick across her uncrossed ankles, and her knees as far apart as her skirt allows.

"We're only just out of the city."

"This line's terrible. It's single track most of the way, the train has to go off into a siding for the other train to pass. Yesterday it did that and we waited for hours. No one knew what had happened. I watched the sunflowers. I could see them turning, that's how long we were there, and the heat was terrible, not a puff of wind. I didn't think it was safe to leave the train, so I just closed my eyes, and fantasised about those cold showers you get on beaches."

I'm an acknowledged expert on sunflowers, and fear that I might launch into a lecture. As the silence extends awkwardly, I can think of nothing else to say, so I tell her about how Van Dyck used sunflowers to symbolise his patrons' loyalty to the king. Then people used them to symbolise a similar subservience to Van Gogh. A field of sunflowers is like Warhol's duplicated trademarks.

"You don't sound like a businessman", she says.

She's right. Why do people lie? A child's first lie is a breakthrough, a realisation that there's a gap between self and others. Lies can continue being used to establish that difference, to gain advantage in some other way, or just for fun. I arrived in Casablanca three days ago, early for a Semiotics conference. I'd arranged some slack time in case the planes were bad or I got a tummy bug. I decided to take a train, not because I wanted to go anywhere in particular, more to see the country. This is the joy of train journeys — you know the beginning and the end, but the rest is a continual surprise. At school I was taught that the engine was the verb, that nouns were pulled along by it, and that every train needed a guard's van; a full stop. Trains are a universal language. Just as railways hug the valleys, so thought needs nouns and verbs. The paraphanelia of signal boxes, level crossings and lost property offices spontaneously developed across the world. All railways have the same deep grammar, give or take a gauge. Polyglot India has 5' 6", 1 metre, 2' 6" and 2' gauges.

In this country the contrast between the capital and countryside is most extreme — the city's minarets, markets and irrigated courtyards, then beyond, this desert: horizontal, female, rolling dunes. Naranj. Once goddesses ruled. Then, thousands of years ago, the first city grew and gods took over. Goddesses became the consorts of warriors or were demoted to vegetable deities, naked until about the sixth century. Cities are vertical, full of straight-lines, ruled by straight-talking men. St Paul and Aristotle taught that women should be silent. Only crones natter.

"I read it in a book. I don't have much to do in the evenings you see."

"Ah, the strong silent type."

One test of an author's knowledge of his characters is to ask what they carry in their pockets, what songs they hum, what programs they stay in for. I carry pen and paper, hum 'Streets of London', and watch Marlon Brando bios. Now that I'm coming clean I should add that I know this woman too. While preparing for this trip, I read the previous conference proceedings, partly to look at the photographs so that I could put names to faces. In one photo taken at the final meal, Dr Rees was shown with, according to the caption, his wife. It was in Hawaii, and she was wearing the full outfit—grass-skirt and a flower necklace. When his wife said to me that she worked in an embassy, I was surprised. It was a fact that I could easily check up on. If she wanted anonymity, why not say that she's a tourist? After all, it's the truth. I tried to recall if there'd been any gossip about Rees. I've never met him, but his theory of two-dimensional grammar has shot him to fame. We've crossed swords in the odd periodical, my deep grammar cutting through his parsed landscapes.

She runs through the usual subjects. We negotiate towards enlightened PC western positions on politics, tourism, global warming, 9/11—establishing roles that we'll play for the rest of the journey, then tacitly agree on another pause as if pacing ourselves. I recline as far back as I can. I'm drifting away when her foot rests against mine.

"Sorry" she says, and withdraws it.
I smile, but don't open my eyes. I suspect she's checking my sexual orientation. An Englishman in his twenties, unmarried in North Africa—well, you can put two and two together. A shame, because otherwise there'd be a satisfying inevitability about the plot: gaining physical revenge over my intellectual rival Rees. Perhaps afterwards she'd accompany her husband to the 'Grammar of Dimensions' session, it being part of the deal that in public they should behave like a happy couple. When my name's announced he'd nudge her, saying "here's that clueless jerk I was telling you about". Then she sees who I am, her lie made flesh. At the coffee break, Rees would come over to congratulate me. "Incisive", he'd say, (meaning "Simplistic") "I don't think you've met my wife. Mary, this is Dominic Shaw". This would be the story's make-or-break moment. What should I say? How could I humiliate him without harming her? But it's all academic. Not only is my paper entitled 'Transgendered Infiltration of Fractal Grammars' but I'm the gay rep for the National Union of Lecturers, to which he belongs.

Suppose we did construct an eternal triangle—husband, wife and lover. I'm not saying it's impossible; I'm sure there are ways I could satisfy her if she insisted. Indeed, my tendencies would add a certain piquancy, making the usually isosceles triangle more regular. But there's another triangle I'm interested in where the trust between Writer and Text is undermined by the Reader who, seduced by the text, betrays the Author who thought the text was his forever. How can the author stake his claim? By closing the gap between himself and the text using confessionalism and self-exposure. I could so easily have tied up the plot by denying my sexuality, by asking about her fantasies, but I chose sincerity over pattern. I hope you reward my honesty.

Ticket inspectors need to be physically imposing here. Ours is no exception. He blocks out the sun as he squeezes along the corridor, fills our compartment and checks our tickets. His "Merci" reminds me how colonialism survives longest on the railways. She locks the door behind him, yanks down the blinds and stands before me.

"There's something you should know", I say.

She does a half-turn slowly, almost balletically, the sun caressing her contours, then she kneels, and leans forward on her seat. I do nothing.

"Don't worry Dom, I'll make it easy for you" she says, raising her backside towards me, pulling up her dress, "just use your imagination."

"But what will I say in the coffee break?"

"How about 'Pretty as a sunflower'?"

DREAMS

My parents' loft is full of broken pieces of my childhood. There's a suitcase of *Rupert* annuals with sellotaped spines. The annuals included origami instructions—a historic breakthrough for the British Origami Society. When there was a bird in a story, they had instructions to make a bird with flapping wings, as if the bird could escape from the printed page. Rupert grew with me. Before I could read I could follow the plot because each page has 4 pictures. There are no speech bubbles; beneath each picture is a rhyming couplet that my mother read to me. At the foot of each page is prose that I read again and again when I was old enough. Now he's going to be in my thesis. On some covers he has white fur, on others brown. He has a bear's head. His friends are pigs, badgers, and children. It's a multicultural paradise, though to be honest they all wear tweeds and quaff lemonade, and Podgy Pig's rather greedy. In the 1990s, after pressure from the States, Golly became a cowboy—horseless of course. The real world was never far away. Debates have raged over the profession of Rupert's father. He's always at home smoking a pipe and reading a paper. Maybe he's a postman, a lecturer, an author, or even unemployed—why not? Rupert had no siblings—few child characters have—but at least he has both parents. So have I. They're happily retired in Southend, pleased that I've settled down at last.

For a while I was an *Asterix* boy too. My parents bought me every book, some in French. I went to the library today and found the *Mission Cleopatra* DVD for my thesis. I'm playing it on my laptop in bed rather than get up and face another Sunday. Asterix has a sense of community but little family life. There's nothing much of that in *Tintin* either. He was a reporter like his creator. In fact, Hergé and Paul de Man the deconstructionist both wrote for the same Nazi Belgium newspaper. To publicise the first book, a boy was hired, dressed like Tintin, to get off a train at Brussel's Gare du Nord as if he'd just returned from Soviet Russia. That first book contained critiques of communism. Other books alluded to contemporary scandals, works by Balzac, drugs and blackmarket guntrading, but no sex—he's even more British than Rupert.

Meanwhile, Obelix is swooning at Monica Bellucci's breasts. It's distracting, so I eject the disc. Then I remember Graham's DVD. When it arrived last week I was in no hurry to try it. The note asked how I was, then said that he'd digitally archived his old Super8 and videotapes and sent me a compilation. He told me how it's all so different now, how there aren't 25 frames stored for each second of video—only the differences between successive frames are stored. If nothing moves, no space is wasted. You can get amazing compression ratios, he said.

I slip his DVD in. There are the usual self-conscious antics—funny walks, sticking tongues out—then Nigel's front room appears. Early in the '70s I'd spent hours there. It was always gloomy, smelling of dusty carpets and armchairs, looking out onto the terraced houses opposite. Whenever someone walked by, the room darkened. In the clip Graham's excitedly telling Nigel about his new video camera while he's using it. It must have been his first. Nigel seems to be ignoring him, reading the back of a King Crimson LP sleeve. Graham continues his commentary of features, zooming in on the net curtains. I'd never noticed them. Onscreen I can see their pattern of ivy leaves, even the individual threads. I click 'Pause'.

We'd all finished college by then and were half-heartedly applying for jobs. When I left, the three of us promised to keep in touch. Two years later Graham moved to London, writing technology reviews for magazines. DVDs are old-fashioned to him, but he doesn't think I can cope with anything newer. Nigel stayed, killing himself in his twenties. I don't know who else but me he had to talk to. I rarely saw his parents. They mostly stayed in the kitchen with the TV. I could have invited him to stay here for a while. I had the space. I used to take in lodgers, wanting them to be more than just tenants. Things never worked out.

I switch to iPlayer. The BBC are raiding their archives too, showing Janis Ian singing 'At

Seventeen' on *The Old Grey Whistle Test*, gazing into the distance. She blamed her hair for her sad teens, dedicated the song to cheerleaders everywhere. I believed it all then, still do, as she closes her eyes, "Inventing lovers on the phone". I saw her at a 1979 concert and realised for the first time I could love a girl who wasn't very pretty. That was before she came out.

I also went to see Blondie, Tangerine Dream, and Roy Harper. The other guys at work used to read *NME* each week to check who was touring but I wasn't into concerts. I don't recall being sad then, though many of the songs make me cry now. I was living fast in those days, changed jobs a lot, travelling, leaving people behind. I didn't realise I'd lived through the '70s until they ended. Even then I carried on as if nothing had changed. Maybe I listened to too many cassettes while driving. Journeys back to an empty flat are depressing, stopping for a meal knowing that the client you've just softened up for hours has already phoned HQ to say no thank you.

Early in the morning of July 9th, 1982, Michael Fagan wandered through Buckingham Palace looking for Rudolph Hess. He didn't really breakfast on Corgi food, believe me. Somehow, amongst the 240 bedrooms, he found the Queen asleep and sat on her bed, waiting for her to wake up. When she did, she pressed the emergency button. No-one arrived—the guards were between shifts. Once her initial panic was over she found him fascinating—she rarely had the chance to talk to people like him. After ten minutes she phoned for some cigarettes.

The public were surprised that she had her own room. The Duke of Edinburgh wasn't even next door. But actually many couples sleep apart. It's been found that people sleep better alone, though men claim they don't. By then I'd been sleeping well for years. A few weeks later I was at my local bus-stop on the way to the train station and Europe. I was going to Athens the slow way, planning to join a flotilla of boats drifting from island to island. Ouzo on a different beach each night, scraping the yoghurt off the beefburgers. It was raining. A short blonde was sheltering under an umbrella. I'd seen her before—shy, blushing easily, never with anyone. She asked if I wanted to share the umbrella. I still wonder why I didn't ask her out. Instead I offered to hold her umbrella. We talked about the weather, the bus service. After I got back from Greece we acknowledged each other at the crowded bus-stop but never spoke. The chance had gone.

Winter '82 was when the '70s ended for me. I wanted a quieter life, one where I could talk to girls at bus stops as confidently as I talked to girls in other towns. I started working for the council and was steadily promoted between one appraisal and the next. People thought I had talent. A colleague talked to me one lunchtime, said he was going to start a management consultancy, asked if I wanted to join him. He gave me a weekend to think about it. My chance of a lifetime he said. He meant well.

I set off early on Saturday to weigh things up. I thought I'd try the coast somewhere. On the road it felt like the old days when I was two different people—at home a loner, on the road living hard. I realised I'd left one of them behind to rot. The car broke down on the M1. I sat on the motorway cutting for an hour waiting for the AA, watching the traffic, closing my eyes and listening. They fixed it in 5 minutes. I was heading north again, nothing was going to stop me this time. When 'At Seventeen' started I hit the reject button, wound down the window and threw the tape out. From the shoebox of cassettes at my side, I picked up one at a time, transferring it from my left hand to my right, casually dropping it out until the box was empty. In the middle of the afternoon I found a hotel outside Skegness, started writing letters to Janis Ian. I told her it was all her fault. I imagined my tapes been crunched by caravans, travelling salesmen, Eddie Stobart lorries, and coaches of day-trippers, the ribbons of brown tape flapping like seaweed. Yeah Janis, roads like the ocean, stick that in your bloody song. Find a rhyme for ocean. Will "Motion" do you? What about "Flapping like dreams in a potion"? It must have been nearly midnight when I asked reception for envelopes and stamps. The guy said he'd get me some in the morning. I knew he was just being awkward, that they must have had stamps in some office or other, so I pushed him aside, shoulder-barged the first door I could find along the corridor. The glass gave way easily.

    I was in a police cell for just a night before my treatment began. That's where I met Fagan. At first he'd been charged for the theft of half a bottle of Californian White, but he ended up in a secure hospital for six months. Inside he was a celebrity. I talked with him for hours about how Janis Ian had let me down. He told me about the Queen. Real class, he said. He was harmless enough. Like me.

Now they're showing The Corrs' cover version of Fleetwood Mac's 'Dreams'. When 'Dreams' came out I knew that a couple had joined the group—Stevie Nicks and Lindsey Buckingham. I thought Lindsey was the chick I fancied but he was the bearded guy—a bit crazy, they said. I responded to drugs well, no ECT. Within six months I was back my desk. The therapist thought work would do me good. He was right, though I still had some ups and downs. Graham told me about Nigel's death months after it happened, not wanting to upset me.

Many writers had sad childhoods, or long periods of childhood illness. Those who write about childhood often do so to get out of depression. Tintin went to Tibet because Hergé was in therapy and wanted life to be simple, covered in eternal snow. The therapist said I had a good mind and should keep busy, so I'm doing this distance learning degree. Being childless helps with objectivity. That's the theory anyway.

Surprised by the noisiness of the rain I walk to the window. At the end of my garden the greenhouse is being pelted, but it's the metal patio table below me that's making a din. I watch the individual raindrops bouncing off it. I look down at my body. I'm getting flabby. I should exercise more. When mum used to drive me home from swimming practice I sometimes closed my eyes, guessing from the turns and braking where we were. Often, as we turned into our drive, I'd convinced myself we were somewhere else. If I could zoom in on my past, what moment would I choose? Realising I'm naked I retreat from the window, remember about the freeze-framed DVD, the grey curtain. I press "Play".

DEFINITIONS

dure — *to fill*

During lunchtime each Tuesday, Dave would make straight for the Holiday Inn and buy a ticket from the receptionist for the pool which was open to the public in the morning. He'd been going there for months — it was secluded, tasteful, and he knew the staff by name (he had studied their badges). He would change into his one-piece, swim 20 lengths, then shower in the only cubicle. He'd use a palmful of almond soap from the dispenser for each armpit, one for his groin, then wash the chlorine from his hair and let the suds clean the rest of him. After, he'd treat himself to a traditional meal in the hotel restaurant, ready to face work again.

     Today he completes his lengths, returns to his locker, collects his towel and t-shirt. But someone's in the cubicle. He waits.

noth — *to feel guilty*

Nothing is inevitable. Dave's father wanted to call his first son David but he only had a daughter, Diane, who married and had two children. One January, soon after her father died, she cut her hair short and announced that we should call her Dave from now on. Her husband towered over her, so I offered her some of my clothes—a spare pin-stripe suit, some shirts and ties.

someth — *to be a sitting target*

Something is worrying him. He doesn't like his habits disturbed. He starts drying himself without undressing. Someone enters, starts changing, humming. Dave hasn't seen him before. He's suntanned, about Dave's age. "Cold in there today?" the stranger asks, nodding towards the pool. "Not bad", says Dave. "I suppose that suit helps. One of those Speedo jobs is it?" Do men chat up men this way, Dave wonders, the way he knew men chatted up women? Dave didn't shave his legs—they were naturally smooth. He bound up his breasts to flatten them, wore a hand-towel around his waist and stuffed his son's jockstrap down her front. Was the bulge too big? Was that the problem?

kiple — *to test people's affection*

I use Kipling is a litmus test—if students dislike his work, it shows they've let other issues interfere. My childhood girlfriends liked David Cassidy. So did their mothers. Us boys said he was bent and his songs were crap. So when Diane asked me if I liked David Cassidy I paused. Songs like 'Cherish' or 'Could it be Forever' were by some of the best writers around. Dave's not popular with the older neighbours because he corrects each gender slip-of-the-tongue. I feel awkward when I see him in my suit chatting to my wife but I don't fantasise about it. "Cassidy's okay", I said.

gruel — *to make a little go a long way*

Dave's finding the wait gruelling. He's wondering whether in the future he should come on a different day. "I like a bit of gentle breaststroke" says the stranger, "What about you?". The shower stops. No one comes out of the cubicle. He hears dripping. Then a young man emerges making no attempt to hide himself. Dave glances—he's become curious about men's bodies, the details. Dave's not sure how to break away from the stranger's conversation, ends up rushing with a shirt and towel to the cubicle, locking himself in and enacting his ritual. His worries rinse away under the hot water. He doesn't come out until the changing room sounds empty.

dumple — *to disguise oneself*

"Dumpling?" asks the waiter. "Yes" says Dave. He's treated with respect here, away from his oppressive workplace. He's never felt quite at home in the south, its supposed tolerance merely indifference. He doesn't define himself by his chromosomes or hormones, it's not a sexual thing. He knows people will respond to him according to how he looks, so he cares about his appearance. He avoids excitement because his voice goes shrill. He's developed a convincing laugh.

pudd — *to waste time*

He's finished pudding and is on his way out when the manager approaches. "Excuse me, sir. Can I have a little word?" "Of course Mr Williams". They walk into an office by reception. "We've valued your custom over the last few months but I think it's time you found somewhere else to swim. We have our clients to consider, you see sir. I hope you understand." He hands Dave an envelope. "Here are some vouchers for the restaurant with our compliments."

unfail — *to fake victory*

"Goodbye sir" says the receptionist with unfailing politeness as Dave passes. "Goodbye Matthew", Dave replies, dropping the envelope into a bin. "By the way", he adds, "I'm Dave".

FRACTALS

This week while I'm home on holiday I'm going to write a story. I won't get a better chance—the papers say it's a White Hell outside. What I'm keen to avoid is pretending to escape writer's block by writing about it. I won't write about myself either because, as everyone knows, things don't become more real just because they're written down. Each day I shall get up early, have a black coffee with buttered toast, re-write for two gruelling hours, take a break, then start again at 7pm. I shall follow that schedule ruthlessly, starting tomorrow.

This afternoon I prepare by walking to the newsagents with pen and paper. The snow's compacted and slippery, having melted and frozen overnight. People have already strung Christmas lights on their houses, flickering in complex sequences. Sometimes there's a semblance of movement along the strands. When I focus on one bulb at random, watching it going off and on, the illusion disappears. I pass an old couple cautiously edging forward, arm-in-arm like in a three-legged race that they know they won't win now; they just want to finish. If they fall and break a limb there's little hope for them.

"What's up with the council?" the man says to his wife, "Ain't they never heard of salt?"

I stop to write it down. The newsagent's empty of customers. Inside the door there's a puddle where people have stamped snow from their shoes. By the magazine racks *The Daily Mail* pile is the highest — today that's as good as any reason to buy it.

No-one's at the bus-stop as I walk back, not even the woman. I sometimes watch The Carpenters on YouTube. People have forgotten them but Karen and thingy, her brother, sold a hundred million records. One morning out of the blue she was found dead from anorexia. Watching the clips I like to think that I can see the early signs — I don't mean the obvious ones like the lyrics ("no-one ever cares if I should live or die") or the skinny arms and sharp cheekbones, but the eyes. The bus-stop woman has those eyes, beautiful and dark, fathomless. She's delicately freckled — Irish probably. I've never heard her, but I bet her voice is beautiful too.

Karen's voice was so gentle she could only sing in public if she had a microphone. I'm shy as well. I saw the woman alone once. It was raining and she had a yellow umbrella. I could have queued beside her waiting to be invited under. Instead I hid round the corner, running for the bus when it arrived. I like rain. I was at a cheap Delhi hotel once when the monsoon started, pouring onto the balconies, through the rooms, and cascading down the staircase. The staff swept it through the front door. A family was camped outside. I remember them clinging to each other, watching their possessions float away.

I find myself humming Ralph McTell's 'Streets of London', the one that goes "But how can you tell me that you're lonely and say for you that the sun don't shine?" There's always someone worse off. I tell people that I'm single because I worked abroad for a few years, because I had to care for my ailing parents, or because things never quite worked out. She'll know how it is, I'm sure. She couldn't have a brighter umbrella—buttercup yellow—and that pleated skirt might cover her knees but when she walks it flicks halfway up her thighs. Next time I'll stand so that the drips from her umbrella fall on me. When she asks if I want to share her umbrella I shall offer to hold it because I'm taller. I shall ask if yellow is her favourite colour, if she likes rain, then I'll drop in my Delhi anecdote. I'll ask if she's travelled too. It's strange, our bus stop. I'd expect each day to be the same but sometimes there's a dozen people, sometimes just the two of us. I'll mention that, leave it open-ended.

At five this morning I should have set off for my aunt's funeral, but the weather was too bad—a shame, we got on well. They say that the dying try to hang on until Christmas. Not her—she hated old age. She wouldn't have wanted me to take risks just for a funeral. I phoned my cousin at lunchtime. He said that they had trouble at the chapel because the doors had frozen shut. She'd have seen the funny side. My cousin's family are my only surviving relatives. I get his little kids lavish presents. You don't have to believe in Santa to enjoy the look in their eyes. Not that I see them often; they live far away. To be honest I don't see many people—that's why I have to make the most of my chances. When the woman's bus arrives through the rain to interrupt our first conversation, I'll say "I might see you tomorrow. Goodbye". No, if I say that she'll just say "Bye" in return. It's better to end with "I might see you tomorrow, then?" to force her into an answer. And I must remember to ask for her name and tell her mine, show her that I'm sensitive and observant, that there's more to me than meets the eye.

Home again, I sip a tea, idly cutting random sentences from the *Mail*, adding the scrap of paper in my pocket to the pile. All I need now is some excuse not to pick them at random. I want a character whose acts have motivation. It's strange how characters are described using words made of characters. Letters, even those to Santa, are written using words made of letters. Come to think of it, paper's made of wood from trees in a wood. How can I make use of that observation, or of how it's not the cold that's so dangerous, it's the alternation of hopes and disappointments? A knock at the door startles me.

"Excuse me sir, but I'm planning to stand in the local election. I think I can do better than the current bunch of monkeys. Just look at the state of these pavements. It's a disgrace. Can I count on your vote?"

It's the man whose words I wrote down

earlier, braving the treacherous streets to save the world. I sign his petition and wish him luck, I really do. If only I was more like him.

I'm not getting any younger. Nowadays all my drafts shrink to flash fiction. The lyrical ending remains in full while the rest rots away except for the plot-hinges and a sentence of description for each setting and person. It's not such a disaster though — delve a layer further down and each bit's ready to be expanded to fill the void — the broken-handled RNLI mug used to hold pens, bought in Torquay after their first night together; an overheard comment in the canteen that makes him realise he'll never get promotion; the row of sensible shoes by her door — little things that say so much, that say the deeper you go, the cheaper life gets. You see, I think the two states of existence aren't Life and Death but immortality (which for me lasted about twenty-five years, and for my aunt until she became a widow), followed by the knowledge that one's going to die. Really die. Nothing after. And not much before. Even those closest to you are chemicals. When I see people battling, fretting and laughing I play along. I don't have to believe in their hopes and dreams. She'd understand, the bus-stop woman. But writing's different. It's like watching a film — it's not pretending to be real so I find myself getting involved, easily moved. This year I've not written anywhere near enough.

So let's suppose there's a couple with a child. I'll be the father. My sister Sue visits for a few days. She and my wife don't get on (as shown by a few anecdotes). My little son (5? 10? Jason?) asks me why. I don't know yet, it's only a draft. My sister says things to my son like "Don't watch that rubbish on TV. The kids' shows are full of black presenters. They're trying to take over, you know".

When she comes back from buying *The Mail* at the corner shop she says that the owner's "one of our turbanned friends—such hard workers aren't they?" She takes Jason to town, scours the charity shops for *Snow White*—which she describes as "real entertainment". She finds a video. She's got Jason all excited by the time they're back, until I explain that we don't own a video player.

"You'll have to come home with me, Jason", she says, nudging him, "I've got all the mod cons".

Next morning, while I'm still in bed (having sex?) there's a knock at the front door.

"Aunt Sue's car won't start", says Jason.

"Where were you going?" I ask.

"Oh, just a drive", says Sue.

"She was going to take me home to watch *Snow White*", says Jason, aged five (like my cousin's youngest).

"But that's hours away", I reply.

"It was going to be a surprise", she says. "Anyhow, what's up with the council? Ain't they never heard of salt? Well, are we going to freeze to death here or are you going to let us in?"

Shall I tell my wife what happened? Not immediately. I need to plant earlier signs of Sue's instability. She needs to be a spinster. Maybe she's envious of us? She thinks I don't know that before my wife met me she went out with a black. She's saving the revelation up for maximum impact (perhaps the moment when I demand she leaves). Or maybe it's to do with my wife snatching me from the family house just as our parents needed care. I should have gone back more. Too late now. Whatever the explanation, I'll let it come innocently out of Jason's mouth—a throwaway comment that opens into a life-time's disappointment.

I'll leave this draft overnight, see if it sets. Then for two hours I shall tweak it, crispen it up, try not to let too much slip away. The pavements should be better by then—safer, more people around, more words to collect. And no funeral. Maybe the woman will be at the bus-stop—so much to remember: umbrella, names, colours, rain, travel, no goodbyes.

HOTWIRE

Taking the short story for a ride on the wild side...

HOTWIRE is a series of short-story collections published by Nine Arches Press in paperback form. A chance to discover some of the best new short-story talent out there and to lose yourself in short fiction that excites, challenges and provokes its readers.

Since 2008, Nine Arches Press have published thirty poetry and short story books and pamphlets, including titles which have won the East Midlands Book Award and were chosen as the Poetry Book Society Pamphlet Choice in 2011. As publishers, they are dedicated to the promotion of work by both new and established writers, and the development of a loyal readership for contemporary short fiction and poetry. Find out more about Hotwire and Nine Arches Press by visiting their website at www.ninearchespress.com or by scanning this QR Code: